Moose's Roof

Story by Jennifer Maruno
Illustrations by Laurel Keating

BREAKWATER

P.O. Box 2188, St. John's, NL, Canada, A1C 6E6

www.breakwaterbooks.com

Library and Archives Canada Cataloguing in Publication

Maruno, Jennifer, 1950-, author
Moose's roof / story by Jennifer Maruno; illustrations
by Laurel Keating.

ISBN 978-1-77103-100-4 (softcover)

I. Keating, Laurel, 1990-, illustrator II. Title.

PS8626.A785M66 2017   jC813'.6   C2016-907454-4

2017, Jennifer Maruno

We gratefully acknowledge the financial support of the Canada Council for the Arts,
the Government of Canada through the Canada Book Fund (CBF),
and the Government of Newfoundland and Labrador through the Department
of Tourism, Culture and Recreation for our publishing program.

Cover Design by Nancy Keating
Illustrations by Laurel Keating
Printed on acid-free paper

Reprinted 2017

For Ewan

— Jennifer Maruno

For Mom and Dad,
who built a roof for me.

— Laurel Keating

Vreeeeew…bam-bam-bam…Vreeeeew…bam-bam-bam.
When the sounds stopped, Moose decided to investigate the campgrounds of Butter Pot Park.

In a clearing, he discovered a new picnic pavilion.

Beaver scrambled up Moose's leg to inspect.
"Nice roof," he said.

Bear scratched his back against one of the tall poles. "Nice roof," he said.

Squirrel scampered along the rafters.
"Nice roof," she called down.

"How do you know about roofs?" Moose asked his friends.

"I make them with leaves," Squirrel said. "Keeps me out of the rain."

"I build them with sticks," Beaver said. "Keeps me out of the sun."

"I hunt for them in the hills," Bear said. "Keeps me out of the snow."

Moose thought about the rain, snow and sun.
"I need a roof," he said.

Beaver cut branches to brace Moose's antlers.
Squirrel gathered leaves to stuff the cracks.
Bear carted stones to weigh down the flowered
turf top.

They led Moose to the pond to admire his new roof.

Passing bees enjoyed the blooms during the day and an owl came to visit each night.

"I can't lie down for my afternoon nap," Moose
told Bear one day.

"Take one long nap instead," Bear suggested, "when the snow comes."

"I trip and stumble when I walk," Moose complained to Beaver.

"Use your tail to balance," Beaver said, slapping the water.

"When I bend to eat weeds, I tip over," Moose
said to Squirrel.

"Eat some nuts," Squirrel said, tossing a few in his direction.

"I'll try harder," Moose mumbled as he walked away.

Moose listened to the buzz of the bees all day and the hoot of the owl all night. His eyes became heavy, his body ached. He grew cranky.

One day, as he dusted debris from his shoulders, Moose heard a distant rumble of thunder. Clouds blackened the sky. A gale of wind hurled the bees and the leaves back into the trees.

Moose stomped his feet and shook his great antlers, scattering the sticks and stones. He welcomed the nor'easter with his best bugle.

Heavy rain lashed his body and the sounds of thunder lulled him into a deep sleep.

The next morning, his aches and pains had
disappeared. His eyes and coat shone. With the
sun on his back, he ate a delicious breakfast of
tender weeds.

Beaver, Bear and Squirrel inspected the wreckage. "We can fix it," they all agreed.

"NOOOOO thanks," Moose said.

"The sky over my head is roof enough for me!"